The CLASS TWO MONSTER

MICHAEL ROSEN

D1345284

MAGGIE LING

HEINEMANN · LONDON

William Heinemann Ltd
Michelin House, 81 Fulham Road,
London SW3 6RB

LONDON MELBOURNE AUCKLAND

First published 1989
Text © 1989 Michael Rosen
Illustrations © 1989 Maggie Ling

ISBN 0 434 93053 9
Printed in Hong Kong by
Mandarin Offset

A school pack of SUPERCHAMPS 1–6
is available from
Heinemann Educational Books
ISBN 0 435 00090 X

IT WAS A Monday in June that our teacher, Mr Solomons, came in and said, 'Right, we're going to make a video.'

Of course, we went mad.

When I say, 'we', I don't mean the ones who never get excited about anything. You know them. You could walk in one day and say, 'Today, we're going to blow up London Bridge,' and they would go on sitting there like a heap of old socks.

Anyway, like I said, we went mad.
That meant:

André
He can lick the end of his nose and he
can say rude words in French because
his mum comes from St Lucia.

Nicola

She's called 'Um' because she keeps saying 'Um'. You say, 'Hi Nicola,' and she says, 'Um.' You say, 'What's the time?' and she says, 'Um.' She says a few other things as well but she always says 'um' first: 'Um, half past nine.'

Thomas

He's going to be Prime Minister or president or king or something. He can say the alphabet backwards. That's not actually why he's going to be Prime Minister, though. He can do impressions of the queen saying the alphabet backwards: 'Z,Y,X,W . . .' Oh blow it, it doesn't look funny written down, but it *sounds* funny. You try it. 'Z,Y,X,W . . .'

Rashid

He can't eat glue. Well, actually, I can't eat glue either but he says, because he can't eat glue, he can't eat bread. Is there glue in bread? I don't know. My Mum says there's something called gluten: maybe that's it. He says it's in spaghetti, too.

Tessa

She's big and loud, and wants to live in

New York with her Jamaican relatives. She can talk *key jug*. This is how you talk *key jug*. You say the word, *key* after every letter of a word and at the end of the word you say, *key jug*. So, when she says her name she says, 'T key, E key, S key, S key, A key jug.' And she says it really fast so it sounds like this: 'Teeky, eeky, essky, essky, akeyjug.' She doesn't say hallo, she says, 'Aitchky,akey,elky,elky,okeyjug.' You know she starts her name with 'Teeky'? I once called her, 'Squeaky Teeky' and she belted me. Any time you want a belt from Tessa, you can call her Squeaky Teeky as well.

Kin

He draws bombs. You'd better not leave your books anywhere near him or he'll draw bombs on them. His tray is fantastically dangerous. It's full of

bombs. KEEP CLEAR OF KIN'S
TRAY, OK?

So that's us.

And when Mr Solomons said, 'We're
going to make a video,' like I said,
André, Nicola, Thomas, Rashid, Tessa
and Kin went mad. So did I. I haven't

said who I am. My name's Louis and when I grow up I'm going to be cool. I'm going to be like my cousin. He's cool. When he gets really excited about something, he says, all slow and deep, 'Yeah, like that's crisp, man.' He goes to college and, once, I saw him kissing a girl in the street. So I said, 'I saw you kissing a girl in the street the other day,' and he grabbed me and said, 'You keep your trunk out of it, Loo,' – which wasn't so cool.

You hear what he called me? 'Loo.'
Ha, ha. That's all I ever hear, 'Loo, loo, I
wanna go to the loo.' Huh! Really
funny. Well, I've got a way of handling
that. I'm really good at rapping. I can
make up rhymes and so when they start
that 'Loo, loo' business I give them
some real cruel raps.

'Don't try to be funny, don't
try to be slick
I'm better than best and quicker
than quick
You can wind me up, you can
call me Loo
But this Louis Loo Loo is cooler than
you . . . YEAH!'
That shows 'em.

So, like I was saying, Mr Solomons
came in and said, 'Right, we're going to
make a video.'

Don't try to be funny,
don't try to be slick
I'm better than best and
quicker than quick

You can wind me up,
you can call me Loo

But this Louis
Loo Loo is
cooler than
you . . . .

YEAH!

We went mad and he said, 'We're *all* going to make a video except for anyone shouting.' And we all went very quiet.

'Now, listen,' he said, 'anyone can make a video. All you have to do is turn on a camera and point it at something.'

'Yeah,' said Tessa, 'point it at me and I wiggle about.'

'Great video,' said Thomas, '"Tessa's Wiggle".'

'As I was saying,' says Mr Solomons, 'the only people making this video are the ones who are *quiet.*'

'Actually,' said Thomas again, 'what you said was, that we're all going to make it except for anyone shouting.'

'Thomas?' said Mr Solomons.

'Yes, sir?' said Thomas.

'Shuttup.'

'Yes, sir,' said Thomas.

'Right,' Mr Solomons went on, 'a

video is just a length of video tape with something filmed on it, OK? So what we have to do is decide here, together, what are we going to video, mm?'

Everyone started shouting at once.

'. . . yeah, we can pretend to be Top of the Pops and dance and wave to our mates at home . . .'

'. . . I could be Dracula . . .'

'. . . I'm going to make a video about aliens and André can be an alien . . .'

'. . . I ain't going to be no alien. I'm going to be Eddie Murphy . . .'

'. . . who's Eddie Murphy? . . .'

'. . . and we're singing mad songs at the airport . . .'

And all the time I'm sitting in the corner shaping up a few raps that could come in handy:

Years ago they did radio
So now, so now, we do video . . .

'ENOUGH!' shouted Mr Solomons.

'Mr Solomons can't be in the video 'cos he's shouting,' said Thomas.

'I didn't hear that, Thomas,' said Mr Solomons.

'That means he did,' said Tessa.

'Right, I want you all to go off in ones and twos and threes and I want you to spend the next few minutes talking to each other about what you would like the video to be . . . and I want you to write it down.'

Everyone got up.

'Hang on, hang on. Only one problem. Your idea for this video has got to include everyone. Everyone in the class is going to have something to do with it. Don't come back in half an hour with a plan for a video of Nicola's big toe.'

Everyone got up again.

'Hang on, hang on. After half an hour, we choose which one's the best. We'll vote on it, OK?'

2.

I went off with Rashid and he had this really great idea. To start off with, it's the olden days and we're all in prison. We're all wearing these convict clothes and there are guards all round us. And it's like a rapping competition between the convicts and the guards and of course the convicts win, so we all go free.

'And what you do, Loo, is write all the raps,' says Rashid.

'It's a smart idea,' I said. 'Real crisp,' (remembering my cool cousin).

'Right,' said Rashid. So we got down to it. All we got was:

*Don't stand around, come here
and listen
They call me The Prince in this
here prison*

– then we all had to come together, and say what we wanted the video to be.

Nicola and Tessa said they wanted it
to be a talent show. Everyone would
have to do something they were good at
and Tessa said she could do *key jug* talk
and we all groaned. She said, 'Cut it out,
youse lot,' which is what she always
says. Then she said we could do disco
dancing. I said I know what this means:
all the girls get in a line and wiggle
about going: 'Woo woo woo, baby I love
you.' She said, 'Keep quiet Loo-loo.'

'Next,' said Mr Solomons.

Sophie, Laura and Emma (the posh ones) said it could be a fashion show. We could all be fashion models and there could a commentator who would say things like, 'David is wearing a green shirt and black trousers.'

So Tessa interrupted and said, 'Why does the commentator need to say David's wearing all that stuff when anyone can *see* he's wearing it?'

'Next,' said Mr Solomons.

A kid called Robert said we could all go to London Airport and pretend to do a hijack. The world's first kids' hijack. We hijack a Jumbo Jet to take us to Disneyland. Everyone clapped and cheered.

Mr Solomons said, 'Next'.

Thomas, Lee and Carlton said they had seen a film on the telly about making the *Jaws* films. It showed how they had done it all with plastic sharks. They said, 'We could make a *Jaws* film at the swimming baths down the road.'

'Yeah,' said Rashid, 'sharks get into pools dead easy. They just climb in, I suppose.'

'Next,' said Mr Solomons.

And so it went on all round the class: Natasha and Debbie had this idea where girls could do boys' things and boys do girls' things. So there would be a girls' football match and the boys would be walking about looking after babies.

'I look after my sister anyway,' said Carlton.

'That's lies,' said Lee.

'Next,' said Mr Solomons.

Maureen had the idea of doing a cowboy film. Someone wanted to do a thriller with Mr Solomons as a werewolf. André said we could do a thing where this teacher keeps a whole class of kids prisoner because he wants a million pounds. He keeps them in after school, and then all night. Until our Superhero comes and gets all the kids out.

'Right,' said Mr Solomons, 'do you want to choose now or talk about it?'

We talked about it and in the end we decided on something that wasn't really any of these. What happens is . . . no, I won't tell you just now, because first we had to get ready.

We had loads to do: writing the story, doing acting sessions. We did lists of what people had to do: things like, who was going to say 'ACTION' and who was going to say 'CUT'. Everyone was going to take turns to do things like doing the camera or making the monster – oh, no, I've given it away now. Well, anyway, there's a monster in it.

3

By the tenth of July, we were ready to start filming.

Next day, Mr Solomons came in with Lynne and the camera. He says, 'This is Lynne and she's a student and she's going to –'

'Is she your girlfriend?' says Tessa.

And Lynne said, 'No, *he's* my boyfriend.'

Mr Solomons said, 'Do you know what I said to Lynne before I asked her to come and help us, Tessa? I said, "Class 2 are OK but there's one kid in the class who is very, very mouthy. You'll find out who it is in about two minutes." Lynne, meet Tessa. Now

everyone, Lynne is going to help you all
be camera men.'

'And camera women,' said Natasha.

Then Thomas said, 'Hey, the
camera's been on all the time we've
been talking,' and everyone went crazy.
You know, jumping up and down and
waving, pulling loony faces at the
camera and wiggling about. You
probably know the sort of thing. Just
like when you're watching telly and an

22

interviewer interviews someone in the street, there's always some kid there, behind the interviewer jumping up and down and grinning, going, 'Hallo mum, hallo mum.' Why do they say, 'Hallo mum'? Two minutes later they go off home where they can say hallo to mum as much as they like.

Anyway, the camera was on and everyone was going bananas. So Mr Solomons got everyone to take turns on the camera with Lynne, while the rest of us went on looning about. Tessa took it too far and pulled André's

ear off. Well, that's what André said she did. Thomas said, 'If she did take your ear off, André, you haven't half put it back on again quick.'

So I shouted,

CUT!

and everyone went quiet.

Mr Solomons said, 'Thank you, Louis. Well, I think we're ready to roll,' and we all went giggly and excited.

'We want this thing to be a success, don't we? We want to show it to the rest of the school. We want to show it to friends and mums and dads. And who knows? – if it's really good, perhaps we could invite some other people to come and see it. So it had better be good, right? OK, scene one: "THE LESSON". Who's on camera?'

'Nicola.'

Nicola was talking to Lynne.

'Um – how much were your trainers?'

'They were a present.'

'From Mr Solomons?' said Tessa.

'From the Queen,' said Lynne.

'Scene one: "THE LESSON",' said Mr Solomons.

In this scene, the idea was that Mr Solomons was giving us a spelling test. I thought this was daft because Mr Solomons never gives us spelling tests but someone said, 'But this isn't real, Louis, is it?' I don't suppose it was.

So Mr Solomons is standing out the front saying, 'Right, how do you spell ''Cheese sandwich''?'

'How do you spell ''Cheese and pickle sandwich''?'

'How do you spell ''Cheese and pickle and grapefruit sandwich''?'

And we had to put our hands up to spell them.

In the script that we had written, it said that we spell all these ones right, and it was Natasha, Maureen and Lee who had to spell them. All was going fine until we got to Lee. Lee had to spell 'Cheese and pickle and grapefruit sandwich.' Every time he went to spell it, he got it wrong. I mean, it wasn't a *real* spelling test, was it? We told him how to spell it but he kept getting mixed up. Then Lynne said, 'You know how they do it in films? They do this.' And she wrote out the words, 'Cheese and pickle and grapefruit sandwich' in huge red letters on a piece of paper. Then she held it up where Lee could see it but where the camera wasn't pointing.

'Right,' said Mr Solomons, in the film, 'how do you spell, "Cheese and pickle and grapefruit sandwich"? Lee?'

Tessa thought we were still practising it (for the thirteenth time) and she shouted out, 'If he talks about "Cheese and pickle and grapefruit sandwiches" again, *I'm going to be sick.*'

'CUT', said Robert. 'We were filming that, Tessa.'

So we had to do that again.

He got it right in the end.

Then Mr Solomons has to say, 'How do you spell "*The*"? Louis?'

I go, 'Er . . . um . . . does it begin with *v*?'

'*No!*' shouts Mr Solomons.

'I think it does', I say.

'*It doesn't!*' shouts Mr Solomons.

'Yes,' I say, 'you spell it, *v,e,r.*'

Then Mr Solomons screams:

AND TURNS INTO A MONSTER.

4

How does Mr Solomons turn into a monster?

How does he turn into a great, slimy green monster with a huge mouth and hundreds of teeth?

Well, actually, it's all done on a machine at Lynne's college.   First we filmed Mr Solomons going mad, yelling *'Wrong, wrong,* WRONG!'

Then we filmed lots of pictures of us looking at Mr Solomons with really frightened looks on our faces. And then we filmed the giant monster we had made (with Mr Solomons, Rashid, Sophie, and Maureen inside). Then at Lynne's college we took all these bits of film and mixed them up so that it really looked like Mr Solomons was turning into a great big green slimy monster. And then, the next bit is that the monster roars,

RIGHT. Now I'm going to eat you!

What was supposed to happen now, was Carlton had to start crying, Tessa had to throw her head down on to her arms and Lee had to say, 'Oh no, oh no, oh no.'

This was the hardest bit so far.

Carlton just couldn't pretend to cry. He kept trying, but all he could do was wrinkle up his nose and all that looked like was that he had just smelt something really bad.

So we got Thomas to do it – but when he did it, it sounded like an old goat.

Then it came to Tessa's bit. She dropped her head down on to her arms, looking really sad and scared, but she banged her nose on the table and burst into tears. Trouble was, everyone thought it was really good acting until we saw her nose bleeding. So we got over that all right; but then it came to Lee saying, 'Oh no.'

Oh no, oh no, oh no.

Now, you wouldn't think anyone could forget how to say, 'Oh no,' would you?

Sophie says, 'ACTION!' and Lee says, 'What do I say, again?'

'You say, "Oh no," and you say it three times, OK?'

'ACTION,' says Sophie. (This was her big chance at being director before climbing back into the great big green slimy monster.)

'ACTION!' says Sophie again, because Lee is just sitting there like a doughnut.

'Er . . . er . . . three times,' says Lee.

'Stop, stop it,' says Sophie. 'Look, Lee, you do it like this, "Oh no, oh no, oh no!" Right? ACTION!'

And Lee says, 'Oh,' and starts laughing.

'Look here Lee, it's NOT FUNNY.
Don't muck about. Don't spoil it. This is
your last chance or you've had it.
ACTION!'

So Lee says, 'Oh no, oh no –' and
then he burped. A great big burp.

'Right, that's it, isn't it, sir?' said
Sophie. 'He's out of it isn't he, sir?

Lee got up and shuffled away, so I did
that bit instead of him and I was
GREAT. I looked really terrified. I
opened my mouth up really big, just
like they look in horror films.

(By the way, if anyone reading this
makes horror films and you need
someone to say, 'Oh no, oh no, oh no!'
then write to me. I'm brilliant.)

Next thing to happen, is the monster
starts eating children. We had made the
monster's arms with broom sticks inside
its great green slimy arms, so that

Mr Solomons could move them about while Sophie and Maureen moved its great big green slimy jaws. Rashid stood behind as its great big green slimy back legs.

Now, the great big green Mr Solomons monster starts marching towards André. It made growling

noises. André screamed. The great big green slimy jaws closed round André's head and a few moments later André disappeared into the monster's great big green slimy mouth–helped by Mr Solomons heaving on André's arms from inside. It looked fantastic.

The rest of us screamed. We rushed away from it and into the corner as far away from it as we could. We huddled together looking scared. The monster sat down. It looked content.

'Maybe it's full up,' we said.

'Perhaps we're OK for a bit, eh?'

'Until it gets hungry again.'

'I wonder which one of us it's going to eat next . . .?'

'I'm going,' said Tessa and started going for the door.

The monster reared up, growled horribly and lashed out at Tessa's leg. Tessa tried to dash back to join us but the monster got hold of her, and stood there with one leg on her. Tessa was stuck.

'What are we going to do now?'

'Wait here till help comes.'

'Oh, I'm scared.'

'I want my mum.'

'We'd better sing songs to keep ourselves cheerful,' said Natasha. So she got up and sang, yeah, you've guessed it, 'Ooooo, ooooo, I love you baby,' and all the girls got up in a row and went 'oooo, ooooo, I love you baby' with her.

Meanwhile the monster was still standing on Tessa.

Next thing, the other teachers see what's going on through the corridor windows. They look worried. Two of them start to come in and straightaway the monster looks up and starts to eat Tessa.

'Oh no,' said Mr Nicholides, 'we'd better not touch it or it'll gobble up Tessa.' And they both ran out.

Mr Nicholides was very good in this scene except that, the first time we filmed him running back out of the classroom, he had forgotten to leave the door open behind him.

He went, 'We can't touch it, or it'll gobble up Tessa.' He turned as quick as he could and ran *bang, slam* straight into the door. It would have looked great in a comedy film.

5

Then we did the TV News.

Kin was going to be the newsreader but then that great dollop, Lee, says, 'They don't have Vietnamese newsreaders on the TV news.'

That started off a great big row because Carlton said that anyone can be a newsreader and that was really *bad* for Lee to say things like that so he had better keep his mouth shut or he was out of it altogether.

Lee said, 'Oh, no!'

And Thomas said, 'Lee, you said "Oh, no," really well that time. Maybe you'll be a star after all.'

Lee sulked.

Kin *was* the newsreader.

He said, 'A few hours ago in a school in London, a teacher turned into a big green slimy monster. It has eaten one boy and is in the middle of eating a girl. Over now to the school.'

Nicola is standing outside the school talking to Edith. Edith is one of the helpers.

'I'm standing here outside Whitestone School. Inside there is a great big green slimy monster eating children. Edith Wylie, you're a helper at the school, what's going to happen?'

(Edith was absolutely brilliant here.) 'Oh dear, I don't know what we're going to do. I'm so worried, I really am.'

This scene was all really good except for one thing: right in the middle of Edith saying, 'It's a disaster,' Nicola did a great big 'UM'. Thank you, Nicola.

6

Next was the big night scene.

The monster kept us there in the classroom, huddled up in the corner till night-time. To do this we had to have permission from our mums and dads and some of them came along to be in the video. This time we pointed the camera out of the classroom window down to the mums and dads waiting in the playground. We bought some police helmets from Woolworths' and Desmond, the school caretaker, and two dads put them on. It looked so good. There it was, night-time, the people standing around in huddles in the

playground, lit up with torches. They
shouted out our names and looked

really worried. Some people were
crying.

Suddenly, there was the sound of police cars: 'EE-AH, EE-AH, EE-AH . . .'

All the time, the camera was pointing down at the crowd, so Lynne told Kin to keep the camera running. The police jumped out of their cars, pulling up their trousers. (I've noticed that policemen always pull up their trousers after they've jumped out of their car.)

'OK,' says one of them, 'what's all this about?'

André's dad realises that the camera
is still running and he says:

'There's a teacher up there and he's
just eaten my son.'

'*What!*' says the policeman and then
everyone down there laughed. We
stopped the camera and someone
explained everything to the police.

Next scene: BACK IN THE
CLASSROOM.

Things are getting really sweaty now.
The monster is obviously getting
hungry again. It is slobbering.
(Washing-up liquid mixed with flour.)

'We've got to beat it.'

'How can we get it to let go of Tessa?'

'Tessa, are you all right?'

'GROAN GROAN YUG.'

'Maybe the monster knows it's
Mr Solomons really.'

We shouted: 'Mr Solomons, let go of
Tessa. Don't eat us.'

The monster looked up. It seemed to
hear but it just shook its head, (slobber
flies about a bit) and growled.

'What are we going to do?'

'Maybe the monster is going to eat all of us.'

'I'm scared.'

'Yeah, you've said that a hundred times now.'

'Oh, no, we're all going to die.'

Then Nicola said (don't ask how come she was the news reporter *and* in the classroom but it was something to do with the 'ooooo, I love you baby' bit):

'Um, if it *is* still Mr Solomons, um, maybe we can say something to please him.'

'Oh no, we're all as good as dead.'

'No, why don't we try something, like Nicola says?'

'Yeah,' said Thomas, 'how about some of his favourite jokes?'

'No, it's hopeless.'

'Wait a bit,' says Robert, 'what about the mad book titles? The ones he gets us to make up on Friday afternoons. Maybe that'll get through to him, eh?'

So I shouted, '*Falling Off a Cliff* by Lee Nover.'

'Falling off a Cliff' by Lee Nover.

The monster looked up. Maybe it would work.

'Don't sit Down' by Stan Dupp.

The monster slobbered some more. Was it working?

'I Can't Keep Still' by Bob Uppendown.

Tessa tried to wriggle free but the
monster put another great big green
slimy foot on her.

'I've got it!' said Robert. 'Paralyse it
with some of your rapping, Louis.'

'No, no, man, I'm not in the mood,' I
say.

'Listen here, Louis, this is a matter of
life and death. You do it 'cos we're
telling you to do it. Just get in there and
punish him with some cruel rapping.'

'OK,' I say, 'I'll see what I've got
cooking on the back burner.'

'Go for it, Louis.'

I stand up.

The others snap out a rhythm.
My arms loosen up.
And then I let fly:

Now listen to me,
Mister Monster
Mister Slime

My name's Louis and I ain't
got much time

You think you're flash,
you think you're great

ut I'm a diamond class
rapper,
make no mistake

59

You shape up, to be some
            kinda robber
But you're just a green slime
    lump, with a mouthful
                    of slobbe
You think you're some kinda
            deadly creature
But you ain't nothing more
        than our old teach

We're the class 2 dudes, to fe
    we ain't got nothing
  So get yourself together
    and slide out of here.

60

The monster coughed and slowly turned
back into Mr Solomons, shamed up by
my rapping. It had worked!

We were saved. I was the hero. They were all crowding round me when Mr Solomons said:

'Now where was I? Yes, the spelling test. Louis? How do you spell "the"?'

Just then, Desmond and the two dads in Woolworths' police helmets rushed in and grabbed Mr Solomons.

'You'd better come along with us, young man!'

'What's going on?' says Mr Solomons.
'All I did was ask Louis how to spell
"the". What's wrong with that? I don't
want to go to prison. I'm innocent. Not
guilty, m'lud.'

'Oh yes?' says André's dad. 'Oh yes?
And where is André? Mr Solomons?'

'Yes,' we all said together –

64

So that was it. Lynne had to take all the bits of film off to her college and we each had a chance to go up there and help with getting it to go together properly, and then it was ready to show.

I don't want to sound like a show-off but it was a sensational, A 1, ace, supremo success. Everyone said we were the most brilliant children they'd ever seen and we ought to get it shown on telly. I've been thinking about all this, of course, and I reckon I'll be an actor when I grow up or I might even be a film director. I'll live in Hollywood, probably.

When people come up to me and say, 'Tell me Louis, how did your great career as a film star all begin?' I'll say, 'Well it was a little film I made called, *The Monster in Class 2.*'

THE END

Look, André, Nicola and Tessa have just read this and they say that ever since we made this video I've become a horrible big head and I'd better write in here that it wasn't just me that made *The Class 2 Monster*. It was all of us. 'Shame, Louis, shame on you,' they said.

I suppose they're right.